PILOT TALK

ANGELS Flying altitude, measured in thousands of feet ("Angels two" means 2,000 feet above sea level)

BAT-TURN A sharp, fast turn

BENT Damaged or broken

BIRD An aircraft

BOARDS OUT Brake flaps extended

BRAIN HOUSING GROUP A comic term for the skull

BRAVO ZULU High praise for a job well done

CATSHOT A carrier takeoff helped by a catapult

CHECK FOR LIGHT LEAKS Close your eyes for a nap

CHECK SIX Be careful

CHERUBS Flying altitude under 1,000 feet ("Cherubs three" means 300 feet above sea level)

DRIVER A pilot

GOMER A mocking term for an opponent or enemy

GOO Bad weather that makes it hard to see

GOON UP Screw up

HOP A flight

JINK A quick move to escape danger

MAYDAY A cry for help

NYLON LETDOWN An escape by ejection and parachute

PUNCH OUT Eject

ROGER I hear you

SPOOLED UP Excited

THROTTLE BACK Slow down

WILCO I will do it

CAPTAIN

SKY BLUE

RICHARD EGIELSKI

MICHAEL DI CAPUA BOOKS • SCHOLASTIC

To my cousins, Dennis and Jimmy

COPYRIGHT © 2010 BY RICHARD EGIELSKI • LIBRARY OF CONGRESS CONTROL NUMBER: 2009932555

PRINTED IN CHINA 38 • DESIGNED BY DAVID SAYLOR AND CHARLES KRELOFF • FIRST EDITION, 2010

On Christmas morning, Jack met his best toy pal, Captain Sky Blue. Sky was a pilot.

Along with Sky, Santa brought Jack an airplane kit for the two of them to build together.

Every day—winter, spring, summer, and fall—
Jack and Sky were out flying.
Jack shouted directions.
"Roger! Wilco!" Sky replied in his pilot talk.

Once, just for fun, Sky snatched his buddy's hat.
"Ha-ha!"

But the wind blew the hat out of Sky's hand.

"Uh-oh! I gooned up! Will retrieve!"

Just as Sky caught up with the hat, his plane was struck by lightning!

"MAYDAY! MAYDAY! MAYDAY!"

"Time for a nylon letdown!"

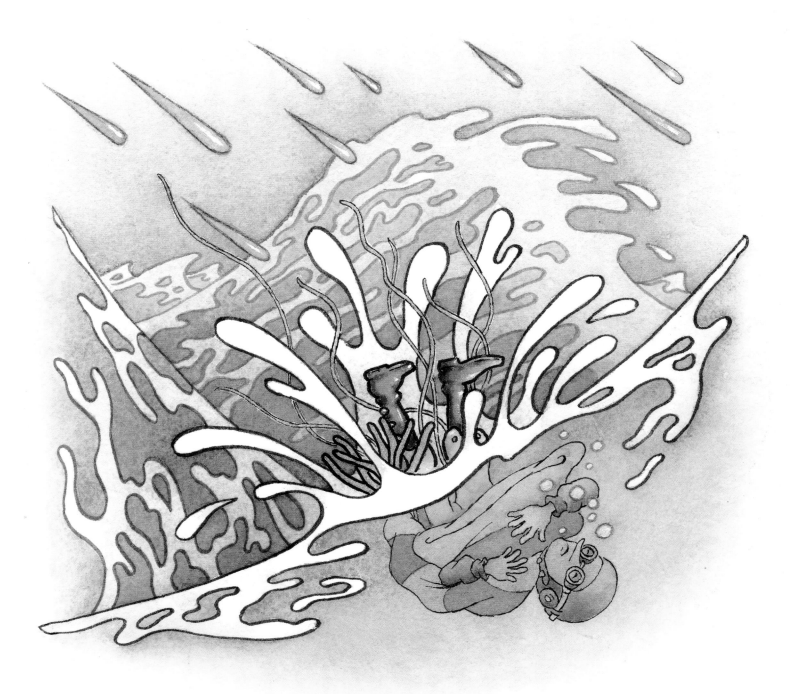

The wind blew Sky far from Jack, far from home,
far out over the ocean, and plopped him down.

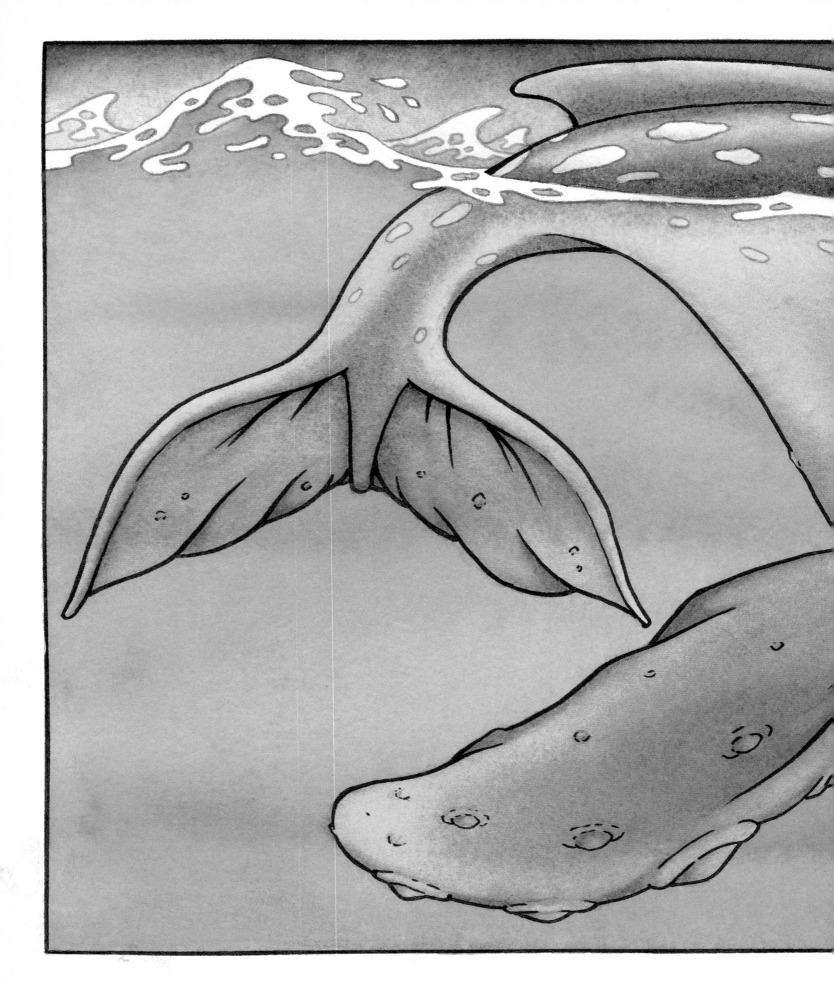

Just then, a whale rose up, took a huge breath—
and pulled Sky right into its blowhole!

"Uh-oh! Gotta punch out of this gomer!"

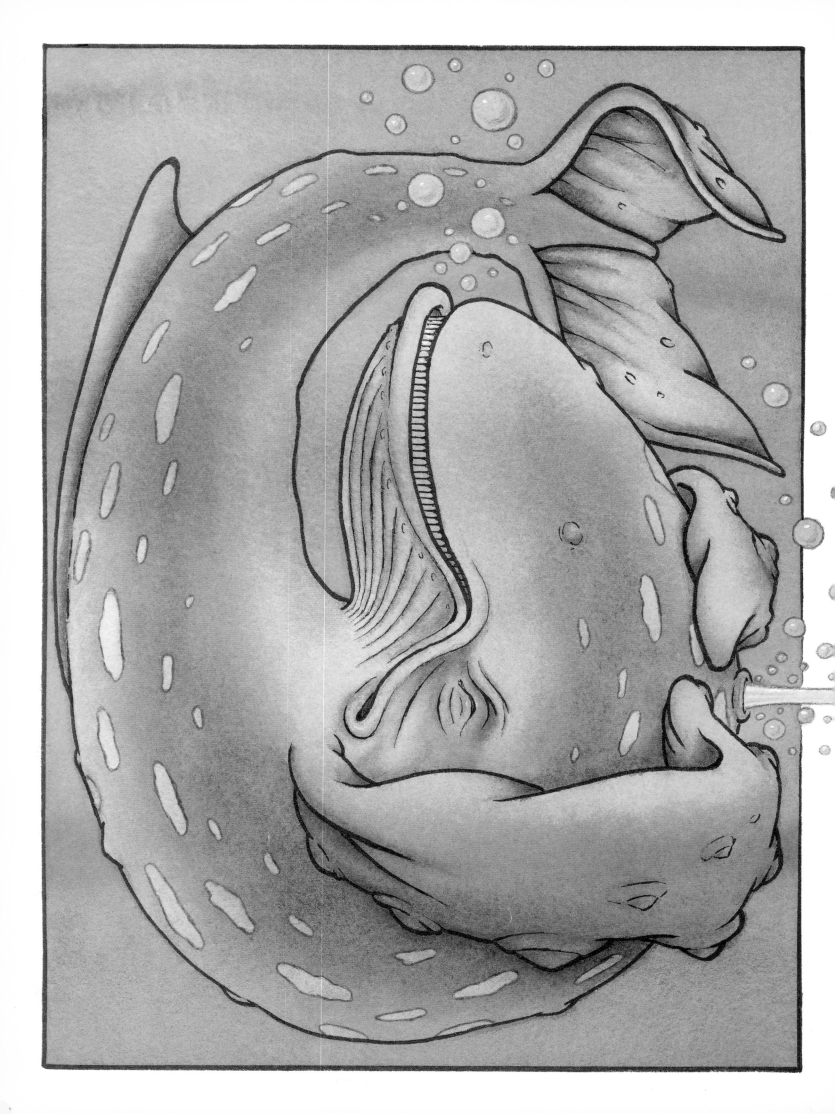

Sky started squirming around in the blowhole,
itching the whale until it gave a humongous sneeze.

"Catshot!"

Sky zoomed through the water, then crashed into an iceberg.

"Anything bent? Brain housing group? Okay. Which way now?"

He wandered along the seafloor, wishing he could find a way back home.

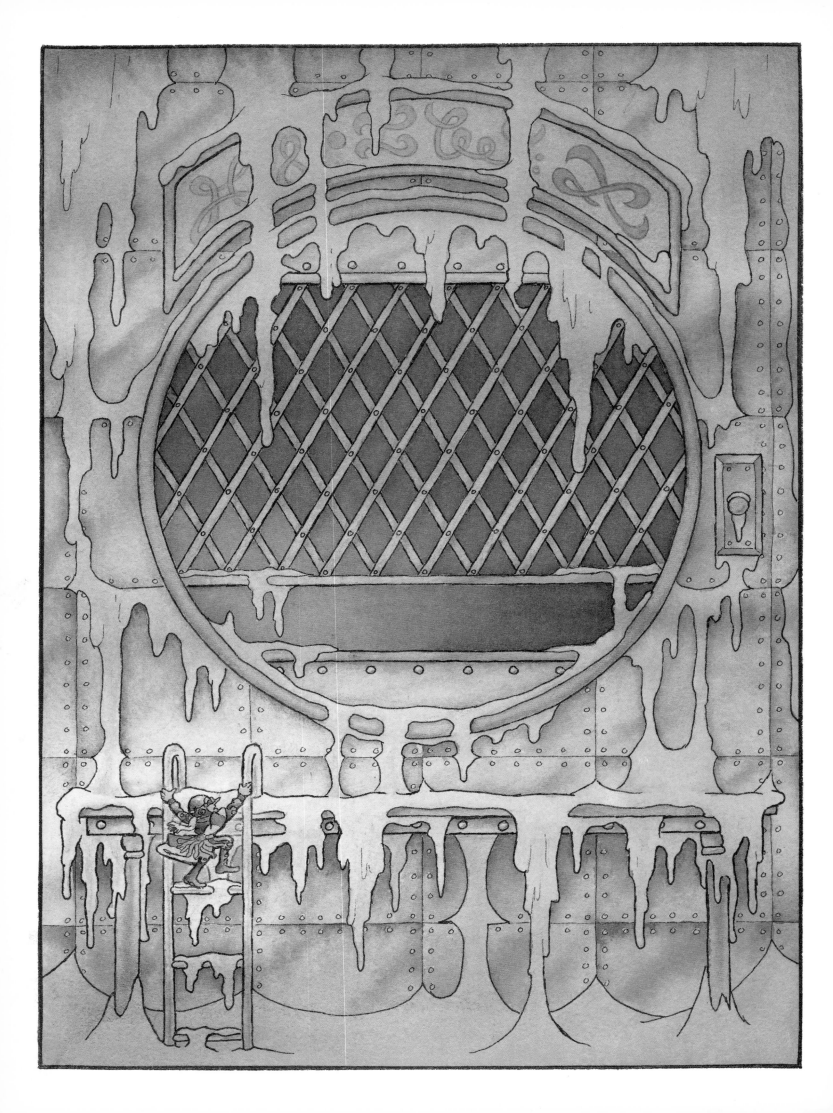

And then he saw something. A frosted, underwater structure!

"What's this? Better check six."

Inside, there was an elevator.

"Easy hop," Sky said as he pressed the UP button.

Up and up, the elevator went. When it came to
a stop, the gate opened.

"NOW I'M SPOOLED UP!" Sky whooped. He knew where he was.

And what he had to do. He had been here
before.

Sky wrote Jack's name on a tag.

"Checking for light leaks," he said and fell asleep.
Sky dreams of seeing the look on Jack's face when
he opens his gift and finds Sky—again!

But Sky awoke to a howling storm. Santa's sleigh was pitching to and fro, rocking and spinning and shaking terribly.

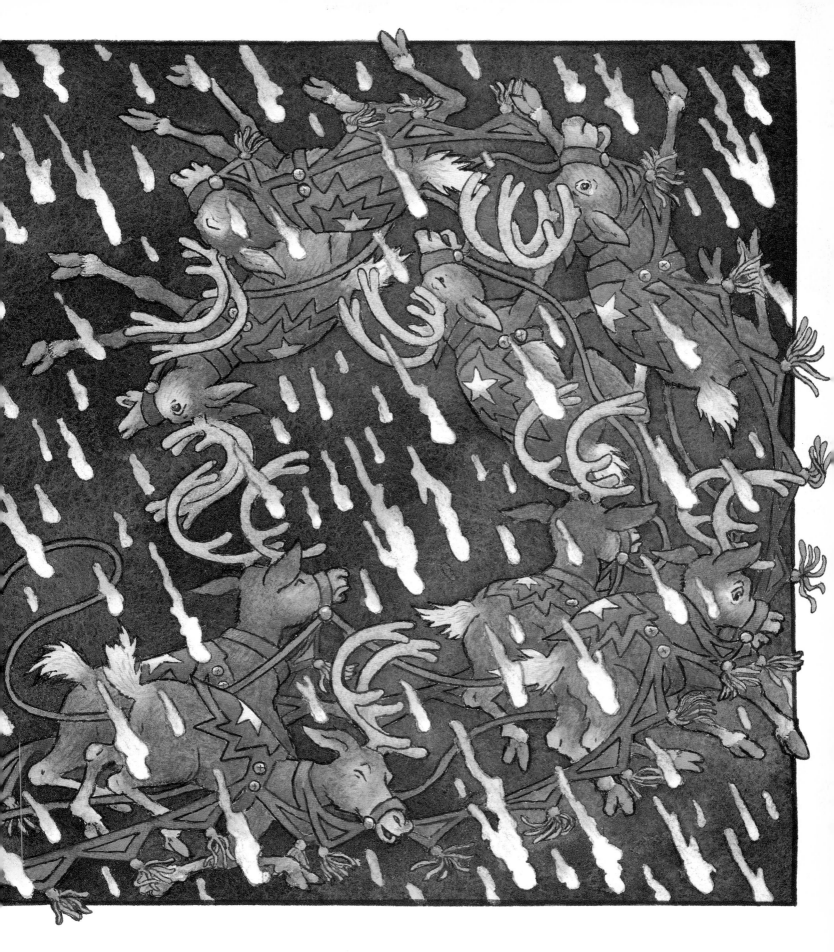

"WE'VE HIT THE GOO! ALLOW ME TO PILOT
THIS BIRD! I AM A PROFESSIONAL DRIVER!"

Sky took the controls.

"GOTTA JINK! BAT-TURN! ALTITUDE, ANGELS TWO!"

"BOARDS OUT! THROTTLE BACK!

CHERUBS THREE . . . TWO . . . ONE . . ."

"TOUCHDOWN!"

Bravo Zulu, Captain Sky Blue!
Over and out.

PILOT TALK

ANGELS Flying altitude, measured in thousands of feet ("Angels two" means 2,000 feet above sea level)

BAT-TURN A sharp, fast turn

BENT Damaged or broken

BIRD An aircraft

BOARDS OUT Brake flaps extended

BRAIN HOUSING GROUP A comic term for the skull

BRAVO ZULU High praise for a job well done

CATSHOT A carrier takeoff helped by a catapult

CHECK FOR LIGHT LEAKS Close your eyes for a nap

CHECK SIX Be careful

CHERUBS Flying altitude under 1,000 feet ("Cherubs three" means 300 feet above sea level)

DRIVER A pilot

GOMER A mocking term for an opponent or enemy

GOO Bad weather that makes it hard to see

GOON UP Screw up

HOP A flight

JINK A quick move to escape danger

MAYDAY A cry for help

NYLON LETDOWN An escape by ejection and parachute

PUNCH OUT Eject

ROGER I hear you

SPOOLED UP Excited

THROTTLE BACK Slow down

WILCO I will do it